parents and caregivers,

Stone Arch Readers are designed to provide enjoyable reading experiences, as well as opportunities to develop vocabulary, literacy skills, and comprehension. Here are a few ways to support your beginning reader:

- Talk with your child about the ideas addressed in the story.

- Discuss each illustration, mentioning the characters, where they are, and what they are doing.

- Read with expression, pointing to each word. You may want to read the whole story through and then revisit parts of the story to ensure that the meanings of words or phrases are understood.

- Talk about why the character did what he or she did and what your child would do in that situation.

- Help your child connect with characters and events in the story.

Remember, reading with your child should be fun, not forced. Each moment spent reading with your child is a priceless investment in his or her literacy life.

GAIL SAUNDERS-SMITH, PH.D.

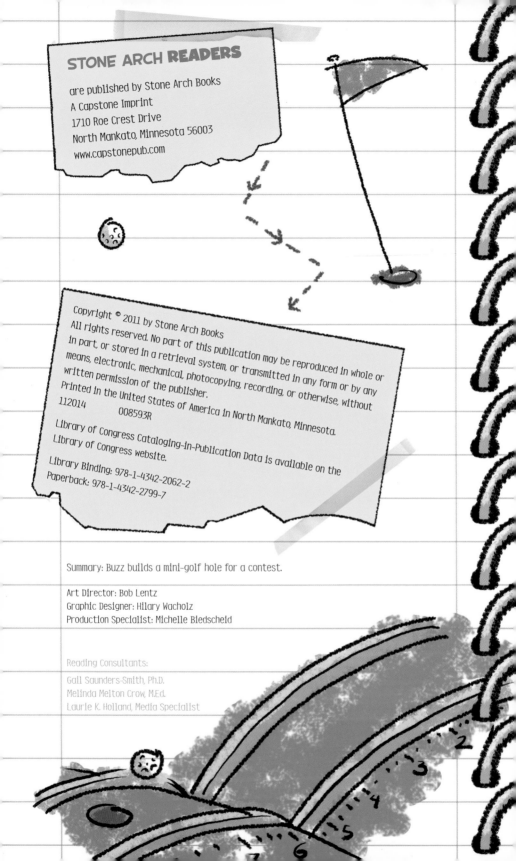

STONE ARCH **READERS**

are published by Stone Arch Books
A Capstone Imprint
1710 Roe Crest Drive
North Mankato, Minnesota 56003
www.capstonepub.com

Printed in the United States of America in North Mankato, Minnesota.
112014   008593R

Library of Congress Cataloging-in-Publication Data is available on the Library of Congress website.

Library Binding: 978-1-4342-2062-2
Paperback: 978-1-4342-2799-7

Summary: Buzz builds a mini-golf hole for a contest.

Art Director: Bob Lentz
Graphic Designer: Hilary Wacholz
Production Specialist: Michelle Biedscheid

Reading Consultants:

Gail Saunders-Smith, Ph.D.
Melinda Melton Crow, M.Ed.
Laurie K. Holland, Media Specialist

BUZZ BEAKER
AND THE
PUTT-PUTT CONTEST

Written by CARI MEISTER
Illustrated by BILL McGUIRE

STONE ARCH BOOKS
a capstone imprint

Buzz Beaker loves
to make cool new stuff.
He keeps his ideas in a
special notebook.

Sarah is the smartest
kid in Buzz's class. But
she is also a show-off.

YUM!

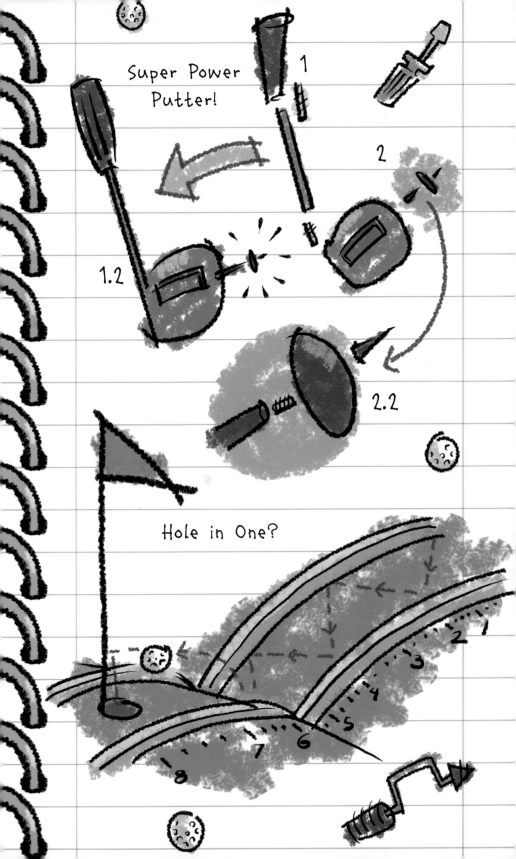

Mike's Mini Golf was having a contest. Whoever built the best new hole would win. The prizes were free mini golf, pizza, and ice cream.

Buzz Beaker loved mini golf.
Buzz loved pizza and ice cream.
Most of all, Buzz loved to invent
things.

"Maybe I can win!" he
thought.

CONTEST!

OUR 18TH HOLE IS IN BAD SHAPE.
WE NEED A NEW ONE.
BUILD THE BEST HOLE AND WIN!

GRAND PRIZE

A YEAR OF FREE MINI GOLF
10 FREE PIZZAS
3 GALLONS OF ICE CREAM

Buzz spent three days drawing plans. He drew at home.

He drew at school.

He even drew during lunch.

"What are you doing?" asked
Sarah.

Buzz told Sarah about the contest. Sarah did a little jump.

"Goody," she said. "I'm smarter than you. If I enter, I will win!"

Buzz frowned. Sarah was the smartest kid in class.

But Buzz really wanted to
win. He kept thinking.

He kept working.

He kept drawing.

That night, Buzz built a small
model.

It turned out great! But would he beat Sarah? Buzz was not sure.

At school, Sarah showed Buzz her model. It had a drawbridge. It had a moat. It even had a crocodile!

"I will win for sure," she said.

Buzz was amazed. Sarah's model was very good.

"Maybe she won't have time to build the real thing," Buzz thought.

That night, Buzz built his golf hole. Buzz sawed.

Buzz nailed.

Buzz glued.

Buzz painted.

Now it was time to see if it worked. Buzz got out his putter.

Tap! He hit the ball.

The ball went up
the plank.

It went through the snakes.

It landed in the funnel.

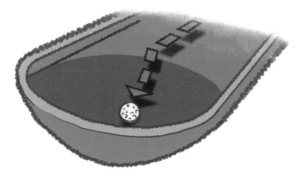

"It works!" Buzz yelled.

The next day at school, Sarah showed him a photo.

"I finished last night!" she said.

Sarah's golf hole was perfect.
She would win for sure.

"You might as well give up,"
she said. "See you tomorrow."

Buzz did not give up. He woke up early the next morning. He went to work.

He added some teeth to
the snakes. He added a secret
tunnel.

Soon it was time to go.

Mike's Mini Golf was busy!

Buzz saw a UFO hole. He saw
a giant mushroom hole. He
even saw an underwater hole.
That one did not work.

Buzz set up his golf hole. The judges came.

They liked the snakes. They liked the tunnel. They liked the plank and funnel.

Then the judges tried it. It worked just as Buzz planned.

The judges had so much fun, they tried it again. Then they wrote some notes and left.

Sarah was next. Buzz watched.

The judges liked the castle. They liked the moat and the crocodile. Then they tried it. All the balls fell into the moat.

"Oh, no!" said Sarah. "The hole is too small. I was so busy painting, I forgot to test it."

The judges tried all the holes.
Finally, they stood on the bridge.

"We have a winner!" they said.

"Our winner is Buzz Beaker!" shouted the judges.

People clapped. People cheered. Buzz smiled with pride.

What about Sarah?

Well, she felt much better
after some pizza and ice cream.

THE END

STORY WORDS

contest   putter

model   funnel

amazed   photo

Total Word Count: 488

LOOK WHAT BUZZ IS BUILDING!